Zak Tidies Up

It was Tidy Day - all over ZingZilla Island.

The ZingZillas were making their Island really, really tidy...

Upstairs in the Clubhouse, Zak was writing a Tidy Song, but it wasn't easy.

Zak would write a word on a piece of paper. Then he couldn't think of another word. So he'd scrunch it up, throw it over his shoulder and start again.

Tang walked in and shook his head, "That's no good."

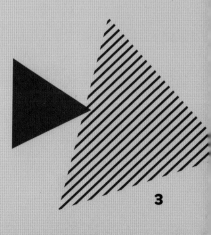

Down in Todd's garden, Todd was busy picking up any last bits of litter. His garden looked very, very tidy.

"Well done, Todd!" Tang said and left to inspect the jungle.

Zak came downstairs and asked Todd what Tang was doing. Todd reminded Zak about the **Tidy Day competition.** Tang was going to decide who was the tidiest on ZingZilla Island. The winner would win the **Squeaky Clean Badge.**

4

Zak dashed upstairs. "I'll never win unless I tidy the Clubhouse."

Zak rushed around picking up every piece of paper he could see. Soon the Clubhouse was looking very, very tidy.

But there was one problem. "I have to put the rubbish somewhere or I'll never win the **Squeaky Clean Badge**," he thought.

So Zak took his big pile of paper and threw it over the side of the Clubhouse.

He was very pleased with his hard work. But where had all the scrunched up paper gone?

That's right – Todd's garden!

Panzee, Tang and Drum were going up to the Clubhouse to play their new song, and they were amazed to see paper all over Todd's garden.

Tang shook his head sadly, "You'll never win the **Squeaky Clean Badge** now, Todd."

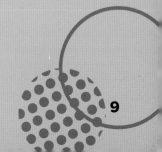

Upstairs, Tang thought the Clubhouse looked **very tidy** and Zak was **very pleased.**

The ZingZillas were all ready to play **the Tidy Song**, but Zak hadn't written the words yet. He'd been too busy tidying!

So, when the ZingZillas started playing, Zak thought, "I'll make the words up!" But the only words that Zak could think of were:

♪ "Tidy tidy tidy, tidy tidy tidy, tidy tidy tidy, tidy tidy tidy." ♪

It wasn't a very good song.

Downstairs, Todd wondered. "Where did all this paper come from?"

Todd tidied all the scrunched up paper in his garden and put it in a bin.

He noticed that one of the pieces of paper had writing on it.

It was Zak's writing!

Todd took the bin upstairs to the Clubhouse to give Zak his rubbish back.

Drum was by herself, playing with a banana.

As Drum was playing with her banana, she dropped it in the bin.

She tried to reach it but she couldn't! So Drum had to tip the rubbish out to find it.

Now there was rubbish all over the floor – **again!**

"Oh no!" said Zak when he got back. He could see a banana skin on the floor.

"Drum..." he said. "Did you tip this rubbish onto the floor?" asked Zak. Drum nodded. She was very sorry.

"Well we have to tidy it up before Tang gets here!" said Zak. So, they rushed around, tidying up.

Drum didn't know what to do with the rubbish. So she threw it over the side of the Clubhouse.

"Oh no!" cried Zak.

17

The rubbish landed in Todd's garden. **AGAIN!**

When Tang and Todd came out of Todd's cave, they couldn't believe their eyes.

"You'll never win the **Squeaky Clean Badge** with a messy garden like this, Todd," said Tang.

He marched off upstairs to the Clubhouse leaving Todd scratching his head.

"I suppose I'll just have to tidy it up again," Todd sighed.

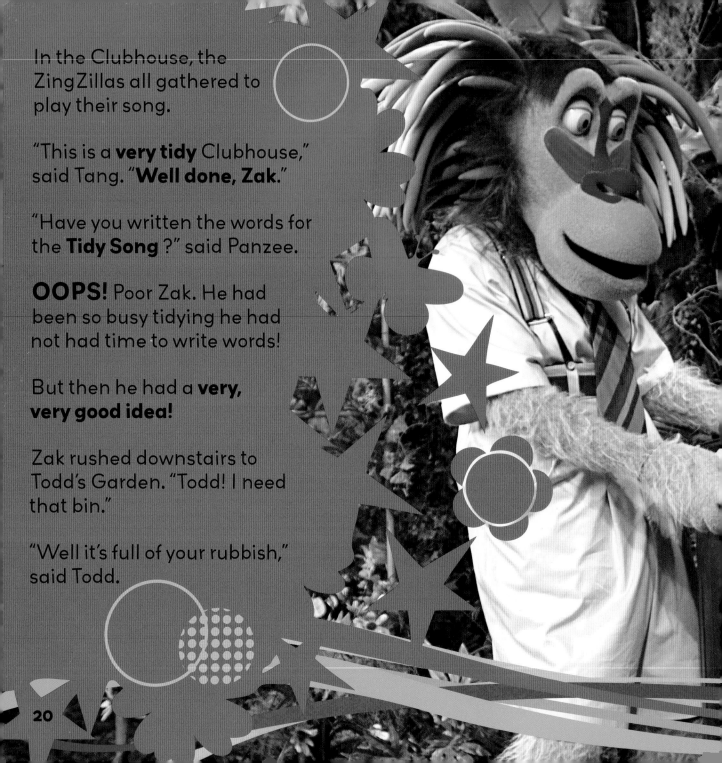

In the Clubhouse, the ZingZillas all gathered to play their song.

"This is a **very tidy** Clubhouse," said Tang. "**Well done, Zak.**"

"Have you written the words for the **Tidy Song** ?" said Panzee.

OOPS! Poor Zak. He had been so busy tidying he had not had time to write words!

But then he had a **very, very good idea!**

Zak rushed downstairs to Todd's Garden. "Todd! I need that bin."

"Well it's full of your rubbish," said Todd.

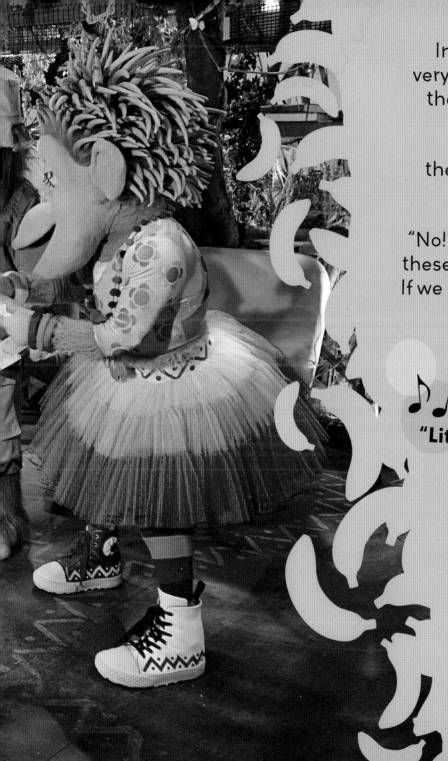

In the Clubhouse, Zak did a very untidy thing! He emptied the rubbish all over the floor.

"Well that won't win you the **Squeaky Clean Badge**," said Tang.

"No!" said Zak. "But on each of these pieces of paper is a word. If we put all the words together, they will make a song!" So the ZingZillas put all the words together and they went like this,

"Litter. Litter. Tidy. Tidy. Rubbish in the bin."

"Well done, Zak!" cheered the ZingZillas. "What a brilliant song!"

And so, when the last coconut had fallen and the Moaning Stones had whizzed round the island, DJ Loose said,

"It's that time of the day when we like to say: It's Big Zing Time! So take it away!"

And the ZingZillas sang their **Tidy Song**. Afterwards, everyone agreed:

That was the best Big Zing EVER.

But who do you think won the **Squeaky Clean Badge**?

Yes that's right – it was Todd. He won it for tidying his garden so many times that busy day!